We ask the author ...

What gives you a fright?

I feel scared when I think someone is following me. I walk faster to see if the person behind me walks faster too. But they never do. It's all in my mind.

Lights in the Mirror

by

C. L. Tompsett

Illustrated by Alan Marks

First published in 2008 in Great Britain by
Barrington Stoke Ltd
18 Walker St, Edinburgh, EH3 7LP

www.barringtonstoke.co.uk

Title ISBN: 978-1-84299-628-7
Pack ISBN: 978-1-84299-623-2

Printed in Poland by Pozkal

I looked round and the red car was still behind us.

It was a Golf like Mum's.

I could see its lights in the mirror in front of me.

"Mum," I said, "that car is following us!"

"Don't be silly, Max," she said. "It can't be following us."

"I know I'm right," I said. "I first saw that car about an hour ago. It was after we had that skid. It was after we hit the tree."

"I'll take the next road on the left," Mum said. "Then we'll see if that car is still following us."

Mum took the next road on the left.

The red Golf went left too.

“I told you!” I said. “It’s following us.”

Then Mum said she was going to stop.

She stopped and the red Golf stopped too.

"I'll go and talk to the driver," Mum said. "I'll ask her why she's following us."

She got out of the car.

The other driver got out of her car too.

Mum walked back to talk to the other driver.

The other driver walked away.

Mum came back to our car.

The other driver went back to her car.

"This is very odd, Max," Mum said. "I think I'd better go to the police."

"Why don't you call them on your mobile?" I asked.

"I left it at home," said Mum.

So Mum drove to the police station. We both went in to see the police-man.

The driver of the Golf came into the police station. A boy came in with her. He had a black and green cap, just like mine.

Mum spoke to the police-man.

“This lady is following me,” she said.

The police-man did not seem to hear her.

“This lady is following me,” she said again.

The police-man looked past Mum. She was right in front of him but he didn't seem to see her.

"I don't think he can see us," I said.

Mum waved her hand up and down. The police-man didn't blink.

"You're right!" she said. "He doesn't know we're here."

Mum looked at the other driver.

"Why are you following us?" she asked.

The lady did not say anything. She just walked away.

The lady opened the door of her car. Then she drove away.

We went back to our car.

"I'm going to follow *her* now," Mum said.

We followed her down the road. The road had lots of bends.

She drove very fast and I was afraid we were going to crash.

"Mum, slow down!" I yelled.

But she went on driving fast.

The red car was still in front of us.

Suddenly the car in front of us went into a skid, came off the road and hit a tree.

It landed on its side.

Mum braked hard and stopped.

“We have to help them!” I said.

Mum got out of our car and I followed her.

We walked up to the crashed car.

Mum opened the door.

The car had blue seats just like ours.

A comic like mine was on the back seat.

A handbag like Mum's was on the floor.

The two cars looked just the same.

"This is *our* car!" I told Mum.

She nodded.

“I don’t understand,” I said.

“Nor do I,” said Mum.

There was a lady in the front seat.

There was a boy with a green and black cap next to her.

I looked at them.

They were both very still.

It was Mum and me, there in that car! Dead.

And it was Mum and me, out here looking in.

So if they were us, then we must be ghosts!